ZU'HAYLA

THE CURIOUS LITTLE FOX

BY: A. SMOOT

A Growing Minds Press creation

Copyright

Dedication

For my precious daughter, A'leyla-
You are the light that guided this story
into being. Through our darkest times, your
laughter and love reminded us to keep
believing.
May you always remember that Mommy
and Daddy loves you endlessly, and will
always steer you toward the brightest
paths ahead.

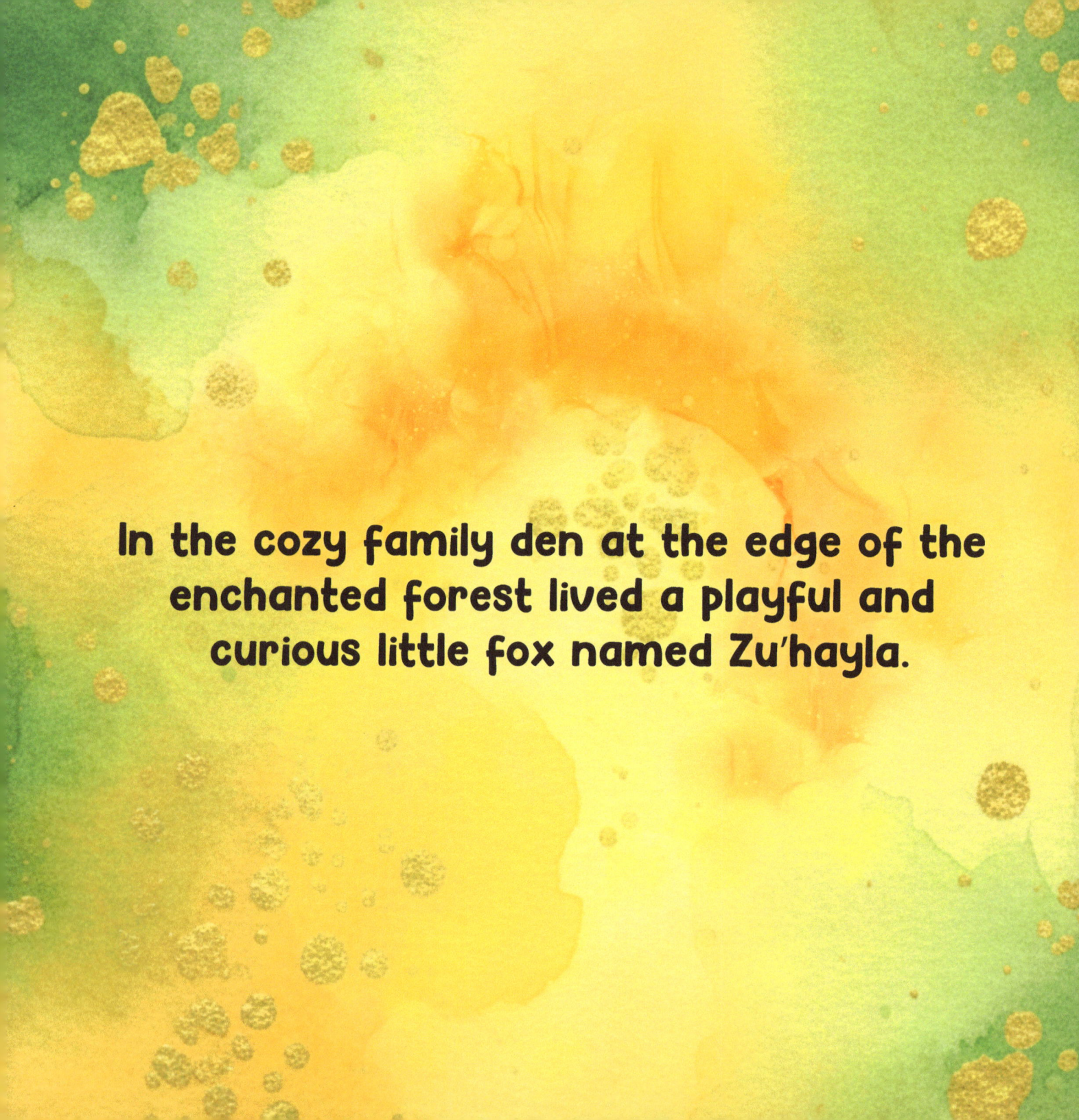

In the cozy family den at the edge of the enchanted forest lived a playful and curious little fox named Zu'hayla.

She loved to imagine all sorts
of adventures.

One sunny morning, Mommy Fox and Daddy Fox were preparing to go hunting for food and supplies for the winter.

Grocery List
- Meat
- Bread
- Blankets
- Veggies

The Enchanted Daily

Mommy Fox looked to Zu'hayla and said: "Zu'hayla, you must stay inside the den no matter what. The Enchanted Forest is too big and dangerous for you to explore alone."

Daddy Fox smiled gently and promised, "When we get back, I will take you outside to explore together before winter comes."

Zu'hayla nodded and promised to stay inside. But as soon as Mommy and Daddy Fox left, she began to feel a little bored.

Her imagination began to run wild
with thoughts of all the fun she could
have outside.

She inched closer and closer to the den's entrance while pondering her mother's warning.

The temptation was too great!
She decided to go outside and explore
the Enchanted Forest anyway.

Outside, the world was full of wonders!

Zu'hayla saw butterflies fluttering, rabbits hopping, and all sorts of insects and animals she had never seen before.

She was having so much fun that she didn't notice the sun was setting.

When it became dark, Zu'hayla realized that she had lost track of time and didn't know her way back home. Fearful and alone, she sniffed around trying to find the scent of her den.

Suddenly, Zu'hayla stumbled and fell into a deep hole!

She tried to climb out but couldn't.
Feeling scared and helpless, she began
to cry out for help.

Luckily, Mommy and Daddy Fox were on their way back home and heard Zu'hayla's cries.

They rushed to the hole, shocked at seeing their little kit trapped, they worked quickly to rescue her.

After returning safely to their den, Mommy Fox and Daddy Fox gently asked Zu'hayla, "Why didn't you follow the rules we set before leaving?"

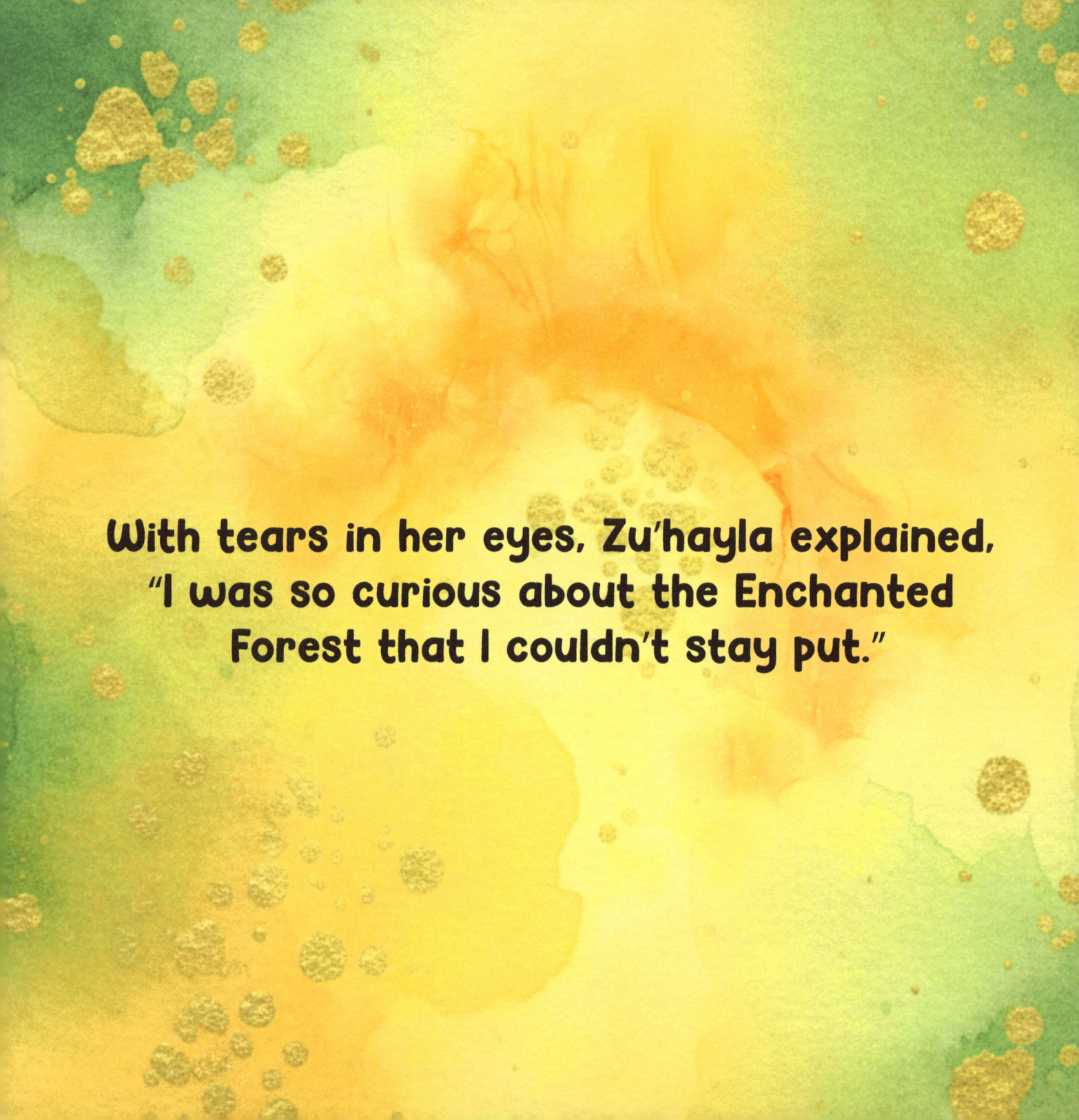

With tears in her eyes, Zu'hayla explained,
"I was so curious about the Enchanted
Forest that I couldn't stay put."

Mommy Fox hugged her tightly and said, "By not following the rules, you put yourself in danger. We were so worried about you."

Daddy Fox added, "We're just glad you're safe. Next time, we'll explore the forest together, okay?"

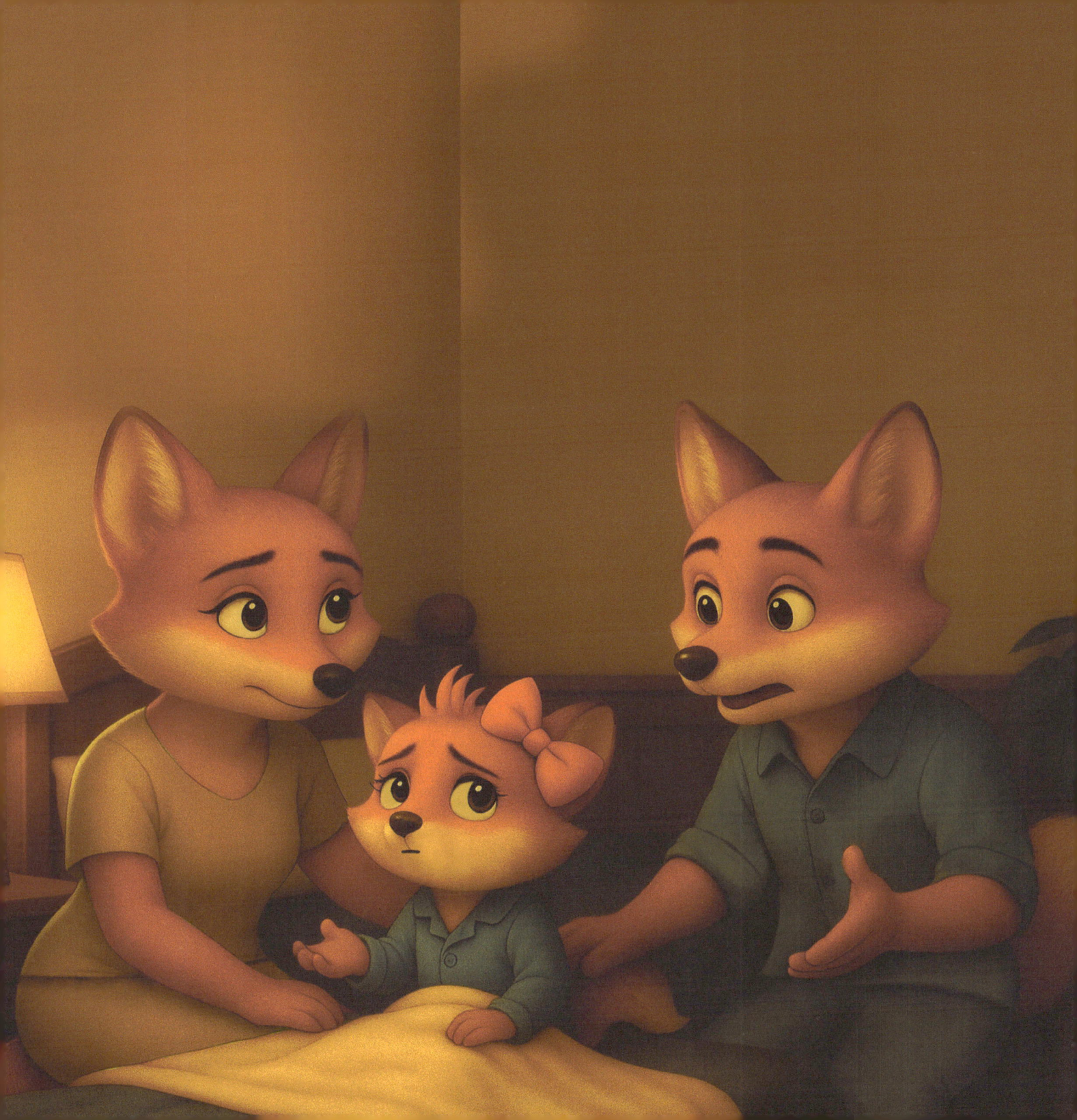

Wrapped in the warm embrace of her parents, she felt safe and loved.

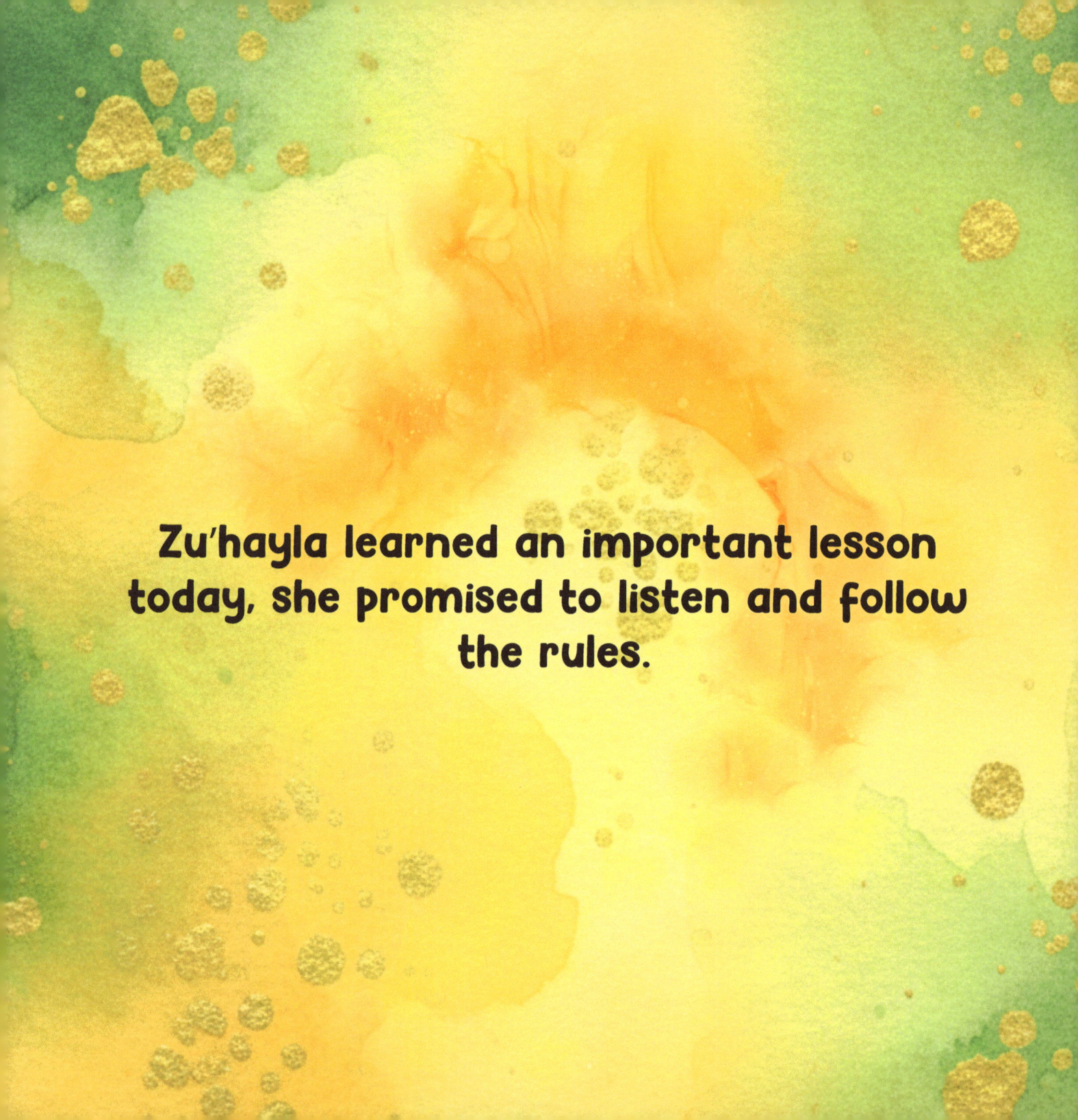

Zu'hayla learned an important lesson today, she promised to listen and follow the rules.

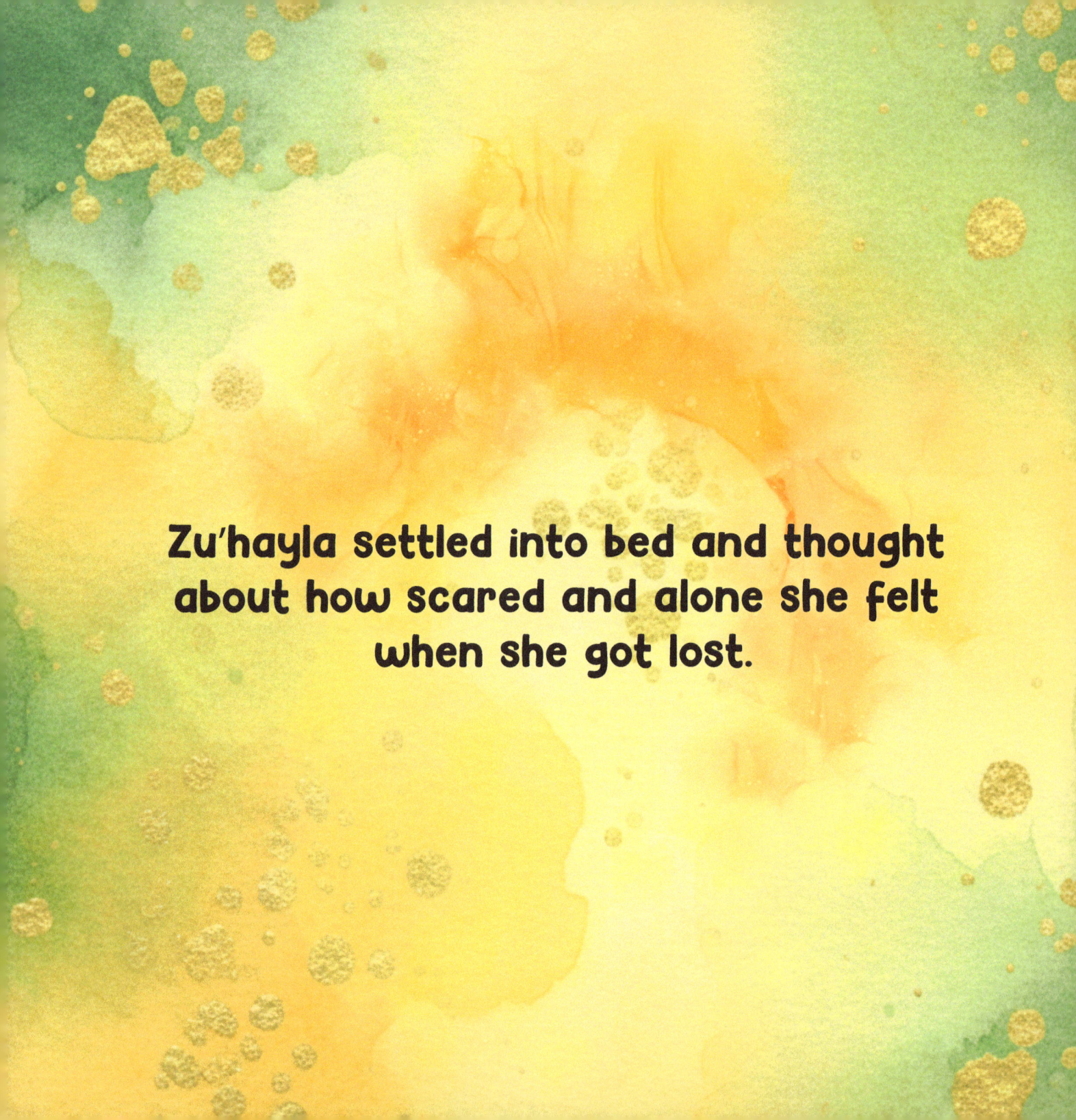

Zu'hayla settled into bed and thought about how scared and alone she felt when she got lost.

As she drifted off to sleep, Zu'hayla eagerly awaits for her next adventure together with her parents in the enchanted forest.

www.ingramcontent.com/pod-product-compliance
Lightning Source LLC
Chambersburg PA
CBHW041356010726
47507CB00002B/178